JESSICA JA

and the

Sugar Plum Fairy

A story for parents to read to children about the real magic of life.

Written by Annie Townsend

Illustrations by Linda Doyle

AnnieVersaries 2022

Poor Jessica Jane has been grounded again
Had a tantrum at lunch. (It's always the same)
She yelled and she screamed "I HATE EATING THAT!"
Threw beans at the window, then blamed the poor cat!
So Jessica Jane was sent to her bed
For the good things she threw and the bad things she said
Hungry and angry and wired to the moon
Poor Jessica Jane was sent to her room.

Thought Jessica Jane "oh life would be cool
If I could make up the 5 A Day rules -
3 Jammie Dodgers, 2chocolate eclairs
Or 3 bags of crisps plus 2 caramel squares
"No mushy veggies, no rabbit food PLEASE
No celery, cabbage or cauliflower cheese
No broccoli, beetroot or stringy green beans
PLEASE give me PINK! I'm tired of these GREENS!"

"I wish that a fairy all sweetness and light
Would bring back the magic into my life"
Cried Jessica Jane as she wept in her sleep
"Please take all the sour and leave me the sweet!"
"So Sugar Plum Fairy please come for a spell
I'll keep you a secret, I really won't tell
Oh ABRACADABRA, just grant me this wish
With glitter and sparkle and a silvery SWISH!"

Then all of a sudden came a warm flash of light
That shimmered and fizzled like fireworks at night
And there between Dolly and Barnaby Bear
Was Sugar Plum Fairy with pink sparkly hair
"I know that you're sad, little Jessica Jane
Your pillow is wet, you've been crying again
So just for a week I will grant you this wish
With a wave of my wand and a silvery SWISH!"

"Oh Sugar Plum Fairy please do what you can
Build me a mansion of lemon meringue
A honeycomb house or a tall treacle tower
A chocolate chip castle that I can devour
A peppermint palace with a marmalade moat
Near a sweet honey river where chocolate swans float
If the weather's not good, I will NEVER complain
If the snowflakes are sherbet and there's raspberry rain!"

"No poisonous Brussels with their green slimy layers
Or squidgy tomatoes, or gooseberries with hairs
No crunchetty carrots, just candy and treats
Just a house and a garden that's filled up with sweets"
Said Sugar Plum Fairy "I'll come for a spell
To bring you sweet magic and glitter as well
I'll make your life sparkle, so syrupy sweet,
But remember the spell only lasts for a week!"

Then Sugar Plum Fairy danced down the stair
Sprinkling words like "SWEETNESS" and "JOY" in the air
She spun around twice like a candyfloss top
And Jessica Jane thought she NEVER would stop!
With a silvery SWISH and the wave of her wand
A sweet scent of honey and then she was gone
And the golden air glowed with a syrupy light
And the moon winked at Jessica Jane in the night

When Jessica Jane then opened her eyes
Her pillows had turned into blueberry pies
"A pink meringue mattress on a marshmallow bed?
I don't think I'll sleep, I'll just eat them instead!"
"A butterscotch bedroom? What more do I need?"
Laughed Jessica Jane with a WHOOP and a SHRIEK!
So she munched all her bedroom, her parents' room too
And she licked all the walls of tiramisu.

Then she stayed in the bathroom for over an hour
As sweet sugar icing poured out of the shower
And she gobbled the bath which was made of banoffee
And the taps were all running with sweet treacle toffee
There was blackcurrant soap and sherbet shampoo
So she glugged it all down and had a good chew
With a crunchetty, munchetty, gobbley glug
She ate the wash basin and even the plug!

Jessica bounced down the syrup sponge stairs
Eating candy floss cobwebs that clung to her hair
There were fudge frosted windows and caramel doors
And donuts for doorknobs and custard cream floors
She threw herself onto a swiss roll settee
And licked all the jam from her toes to her knees
"Now I must see the garden!" cried Jessica Jane
"I'll have pudding outside in the raspberry rain!"

"How delicious," shrieked Jessica, "Even more yummy -
A white chocolate fountain all melted and runny!"
There were butterscotch bushes and tall toffee trees
And lollipop flowers nodding heads in the breeze
A rocky road path wound its way to a stream
Flowing and glowing with vanilla ice cream
And licorice leaves that tickled her knees
She ate seconds and thirds, and FOURTHS IF YOU PLEASE!

Cried Jessica Jane "Oh I'm fuller than full!
I don't think I eat quite so much as a rule!
I feel a bit yucky", she moaned, with a shiver
"So I'll take a quick drink from this lemonade river!"
But the chocolate flake fence made her dizzy and funny
And she then had a terrible pain in her tummy
After gobbling up all of the gingerbread gate
Then her poor toothiepegs started to ACHE!

"Oh Sugar Plum Fairy please hurry back, QUICK!"
Moaned Jessica Jane, "I feel kind of sick!
I'm so tired of hiccups and pains in my tummy
And toothache and jaw ache and sugar and honey
How I miss juicy carrots and salad for lunch
Oh a fresh shiny apple I'd SO like to munch
My face is all spotty, my clothes feel so tight
So Sugar Plum Fairy, make everything right!"

Then a snowstorm of sparkles swirled through the air
And the room smelled of coconut, peaches and pears
There were splashes of silver and flashes of gold
And Jessica Jane did suddenly behold
A shimmery fairy in an apple green dress
The prettiest and cutest, she had to confess
"You're not Sugar Plum Fairy!" she gasped in a whisper
"No I'm Five-a-Day Fairy, her healthy young sister!"

"Oh Five-A-Day Fairy, I'm so sick of sweets
And fudges and toffees and sweet sticky treats
My tummy's so OWY, my toothiepegs ache
How I long for an orange instead of a cake!"
Said Five-A-Day Fairy "Please don't take the blame.
Don't worry your pretty head, Jessica Jane
You thought your life dull and so incomplete
But candies and pudding don't make this life sweet!"

"For the sweet things in life are friendship and fun,
They're fresh air and nature and the warmth of the sun
They're not candy coated or wrapped up as sweets
They're kindness and love and the fresh food we eat!
So breathe in the sweetness, dear Jessica Jane
Run in the wind, be refreshed by the rain!
"But remember," she added with a twinkly smile
"Treats are just fine every once in a while!"

"Farewell Five-A-Day!" sobbed Jessica Jane
"I'm feeling so sad. Will I see you again?"
"Oh yes!", she replied, "On your birthday each year
The sun will turn silver and then we'll appear
But our magical visit will have to be earned
If you're not sweet and kind, we will never return!"
And with a wave of her wand and a silvery SWISH
She flew out the window, blowing Jessica a kiss

So Jessica Jane now understood
She promised her Fairies that she would be good
She ate all of this and she ate all of that
She never got mad or threw beans at the cat!
Said her Mum to her Dad, "Do you think this will last?
Are her days of being grounded all in the past?"
And on Jessica's chart full of stars that she'd earned
She marked off the days 'til her Fairies returned.

FAIRIES RETURN

On the day she turned 6, the 10th of July

A silvery sun danced across a blue sky

Jessica woke to the sound of the birds

"*Happy Birthday to you*" was the song that they chirped

And the air was so fresh with a honey mint breeze

There were green shiny apples on tall toffee trees

And in clouds of meringue someone spelled out her name

"HAPPY BIRTHDAY TO YOU, SWEEET JESSICA JANE!"

And then the sky shimmered with raspberry rain
"Oh thank you dear Fairies!" shrieked Jessica Jane
For flying in the clouds much to her delight
Was Sugar Plum Fairy in a pink spinning light
Then Five-A-Day followed as Jessica wished
With a FIZZ and a FLASH and a SPIN and a SWISH
Cried Jessica Jane "Now my birthday's complete!
It's a Sugar Plum Party with Five-a-Day treats!"

Said Sugar Plum Fairy "We're here for a day
Then the spell will be broken, we must go away
If we don't keep our promises, Jessica Jane,
Our magical powers are never the same"
Then she gave her a butterfly kiss on her cheek
And placed birthday gifts at Jessica's feet
"There's crispy cream donuts just for a start
And caramel muffins and toffee fudge tarts!"

"WAIT!" laughed Five-a Day, "Just take it easy!"
"You know too much sugar can make you feel queasy.
A few birthday cakes and sweet goodies are fine,
But remember this five-a-day basket of mine"
"There's crunchetty carrots and honeydew melon
And freshly made smoothies with orange and lemon
I've salads so yummy with nuts and with raisins
And my cucumber sandwiches taste so amazing!"

Said Five-A-Day Fairy "We have a Surprise

"But Jessica Jane you must first close your eyes

Then we'll fly you with friends to a place far away

Where mermaids they swim and unicorns play

It's a magical kingdom, way up in the clouds

But it's only for children, so we're not allowed

Said Sugar Plum "Now we must both disappear

And you know we'll come back for your birthday next year"

Cried Jessica Jane "I don't understand,

How can we get to this magical land?

It's so far away, I can't jump that high

Why even my apple tree can't reach the sky"

Said Sugar Plum Fairy "PLEASE do not fear,

Just think of three friends and then they'll appear

And suddenly Rosie and Franka and Claire

Were right by her side wondering how they got there!

So Jessica hugged her two Fairies goodbye

And pink and green glitter tears fell from her eyes

Said Sugar Plum "Here is your last birthday wish

And they both waved their wands with a silvery SWISH

And all of a sudden the Fairies had gone

And through a pink mist soared a beautiful swan

The biggest and prettiest they'd ever seen

With rich satin feathers of emerald green

"You're the size of my garden!" cried Jessica Jane
"Oh but so much more pretty than a boring old plane!"
"Hop on!" said the swan "Don't be scared, you'll be fine
We're flying through the heavens all the way to Cloud 9
Then hundreds of fireflies in pink, blue and white
Lit up a path like a ribbon of light
And the children all screamed "OH WOW! This is fun!"
But their magic adventure had only begun!

They flew to a candyfloss world in the skies
With marshmallow mountains and blue butterflies
There were unicorn rides across silvery sands
And they swam with the mermaids to undersea lands
They ran and they jumped across lemonade ponds
They conjured up spells with their own magic wands
And Jessica gathered wild flowers with her friends
For the minute they picked them they grew back again!

And there at the top of a tall lilac tree
They picknicked with monkeys and mauve chimpanzees
And the parrots told jokes, and they laughed 'til they cried
"I could live here forever!" young Jessica sighed
And tiny gold fairies the size of their hands
Taught them to fly off to faraway lands
Where Jessica played Hide and Seek with her friends
But she knew that the magic would come to an end

Then a ribbon of fireflies lit up the skies
And Jessica knew it was time for goodbyes
And the beautiful swan of emerald green
Soared down to Cloud 9, such a wonderful scene!
"It's time to return, dear Jessica Jane"
But your journey back home won't be the same"
They took off with a WHOOSH - oh what a ride!
And landed on top of a chocolate milk slide

It swept down from the heavens like a huge waterfall
But none of the girls were frightened at all
Then quick as a FLASH they're at home on the grass
"Whatever just happened?" young Franka had asked.
"I haven't a clue. But I know we had fun!",
Said Rosie, "Did we fall asleep in the sun?"
"Well I can't remember, but my sides are so sore
From laughing so much!", said Claire "I WANT MORE!"

Soon the party was over, her friends had to leave
Jessica smiled as she pulled from her sleeve
A beautiful feather in emerald green
The prettiest feather she ever had seen
She remembered the unicorn rides in the sand
And tiny gold fairies tickling her hand
She remembered the picnic on top of the tree
And swimming with mermaids under the sea

Then Sugar Plum's voice it sang through the breeze
"Sweet Jessica Jane I hope you are pleased
With your magical birthday you had on Cloud 9
Your friends won't remember but that is just fine
They'll remember the laughter, the fresh air and fun
And that's what's important when all's said and done
So be good and be healthy Jessica dear
We'll be back on your birthday. We'll see you next year!"

That night before bedtime (this also is true)
Jessica found silver sand in her shoes
And there by her side was her last birthday present
Both naughty and yummy and really quite pleasant -
A big toffee apple, shiny and bright
Pink on the left and green on the right
And a flower from Cloud 9 that she'd picked with her friends
She'll plant it tomorrow, then pick it again.

THE END

ACKNOWLEDGEMENTS

A very big Magical Thank You (with a *SILVERY SWISH)* goes to*:*

Linda Doyle for her magical illustrations

Chris Dempsey and Ian Boughton for answering all my questions

Lorna, Ash, Claire and Iain for their encouragement and suggestions

Rosie and Franka for showing me the magic in life

Sugar Plum Fairy for inspiring me for a spell

Five a Day Fairy for saying sweets are okay once in a while

Mike and Lorna for always sharing their sweeties

Mum and Dad for all the healthy meals we had when we were wee

Mum for all the amazing birthday cakes she made

And Charlie the Dog for sitting patiently at the bottom of the stairs

Printed in Great Britain
by Amazon

11353120R00022